D1379346

THE FRECKLE FAIRY

BOOK AND AUDIO CD

BY BOBBIE HINMAN
ILLUSTRATED BY MARK WAYNE ADAMS
DESIGN AND LAYOUT BY JEFF URBANCIC

www.bestfairybooks.com

The Freckle Fairy

Illustrations by Mark Wayne Adams
Text design and layout: Jeff Urbancic

Voices on CD: Narrator, Bobbie Hinman; Music and vocals, Ken Glover; Giggles, Bobbie's grandchildren
Lyrics: Lauren Greenberg
Audio engineer: Jerry Kornbluth - AJRecording.com
Printed in China by Amica, Inc., 07/20/2016

Library of Congress Control Number: 2015934992

Publisher's Cataloging-in-Publication
(Provided by Quality Books, Inc.)

Hinman, Bobbie, author.
The freckle fairy : book and audio CD / by Bobbie Hinman; illustrated by Mark Wayne Adams.
pages cm + 1 audio disc (digital ; 4 3/4 in.)
Includes compact disc.
SUMMARY: In this rhyming book, a mischievous little fairy flies through the night sky, visiting children as they sleep, depositing kisses on foreheads, noses and chins. When the children awaken, they are delighted to see that a freckle has appeared on each place she has kissed.
Audience: Ages 3-7.
ISBN 978-0-9786791-2-5
1. Fairies--Juvenile fiction. 2. Freckles--Juvenile fiction. 3. Stories in rhyme. [1. Fairies--Fiction. 2. Freckles--Fiction. 3. Stories in rhyme.] I. Adams, Mark Wayne, 1971- illustrator. II. Title.

PZ8.3.H5564Fre 2016 [E]
QBI16-600064

Best Fairy Books
www.bestfairybooks.com

This book is dedicated with love to all children who have been kissed by a fairy.
And to my precious grandchildren, who continue to inspire me.

Do YOU think it's true that fairies have freckles just like you and me?

How did they get there? Why do we have them?
Let's find some fairies and see.

Late at night when the moon is high,

and stars are twinkling in the sky...

tiny as a little feather,

one fairy gathers the others together.

She says, "I'll be kissing the children tonight.

I'll be very careful. I'll stay out of sight."

"You stay right here and watch over each other,

while I kiss the children, *one after another*."

“I’ll need to get ready. My warm scarf will do,

and a sandwich, some fruit and a cookie or two."

So the fairies all help her to pack her supplies,

including the goggles she wears on her eyes...

to help her see clearly high in the sky,

as the moon and the stars go whizzing right by.

You won't see her coming. You won't even know.

She flies late at night with just the moon's glow.

She kisses each forehead, each cheek, chin and nose.

She might even give you a kiss on your toes!

And when you awaken and look at your face,

you may find there are freckles all OVER the place.

Wherever she kissed you, the freckles in sight...

are proof that the fairy was here late last night.

You will all be so happy, you won't even mind...

when you look at each other and smile as you find...

the freckles she left you, each magical dot...

a kiss from the fairy who loves you a LOT!

The Freckle Fairy Song

(To the tune of London Bridge is Falling Down)

Verse 1

Freckle Fairy flying high,
In the sky, wave bye bye.
Everywhere she kisses you
There's a freckle!

Verse 2

When the moon begins to glow,
Soon you'll know, she loves you so.
Everywhere she kisses you
There's a freckle!

Verse 3

On your face she'll find a spot,
She likes a lot and makes a dot.
Everywhere she kisses you
There's a freckle!

Verse 4

Counting freckles, fun to do,
I have one, you have two.
Everywhere she kisses you
There's a freckle!